Once a semester, each class in the school has to give an assembly. For their assembly, Miss Beech's class had decided to perform one of the Jolly Plays.

First, they read all of the plays, and then they needed to choose which one they wanted to perform. They all voted, and decided that they liked the one about Anansi the Spider best.

They read the Anansi play together and talked about it, so they were confident that they knew the story. Then they read it again, taking turns to read a sentence each.

The next week, they read the play again with some children taking a part and reading the lines for one of the characters. They tried to change their voices to sound like the animal they were pretending to be.

The mice had high, squeaky voices and the buffalo had a big, loud, low voice. The next week they split up into sets to read and act out the play. They really enjoyed acting out the different parts.

As well as performing the play, they needed to make the backdrop and costumes, and collect the props such as pots, pans, and spoons. The backdrop was going to be a row of five houses, where the different animals live. Miss Beech had some huge rectangles of cardboard for them to use.

The class divided into five sets and each set had to draw the outline of a house filling all of the space on the cardboard. They had to draw the roofs, doors, and windows.

When Miss Beech had checked the outlines, they could start painting. Each house had to look different and show who lived there.

When they had finished, the houses were carefully carried out, put in a spare classroom, and left to dry.

When they were dry, the children added sponge-painted brick shapes, keyholes, and door knockers. Some had painted window boxes with flowers in.

In another lesson they found out about different sorts of houses: terraces, bungalows, apartments, cottages, cabins, and even caves.

They also found out about what houses are made from and how different they are in different places. They were amazed when Cheng told them that some houses in Japan have inside walls made from paper.

Miss Beech printed the lines that the children needed to say in the play and handed them out. Everyone who wanted to could try saying and acting out the lines for a character in the play.

The children who enjoyed performing and acting volunteered to read the speaking parts. Miss Beech told them to take their lines home and learn them over the weekend. Some children didn't want a speaking part, but Miss Beech made sure that everyone had something to do in the play.

The next week, they went into the hall to rehearse their lines and sort out when and where they had to be on the stage. There were a lot of children on the stage and they had to be careful to stand in the right place at the right time.

Next, those who had lines had to try and remember to say them without needing a prompt from Miss Beech.

Miss Beech told the children that if they forgot the exact lines, they should not panic but just say what they could remember. She stood at the back of the hall to make certain that they were speaking loudly. It was important that everyone would be able to hear what they said.

Some of the mothers and fathers helped to make outfits and find props. Seth was Anansi the Spider. The extra legs on his spider body were made from old pairs of black tights stuffed with newspaper. These legs wobbled and waved as he scuttled about the stage.

The rabbits had big fluffy tails and twitched their noses as they hopped around.

The lizard had a patterned costume with a long tail attached to it. The mouse wore a white top and pants with a long rope tail and ears attached to a band on her head. The crow was all in black, with feathered wings attached to his arms and a beak made from cardboard and held on with elastic.

They rehearsed the play several times, making certain that everything ran smoothly. There was a lot to remember, such as collecting props when they were needed, and entering and exiting the stage at the right time.

On the day of the assembly, everyone was excited. They had to wait in the corridor for the rest of the school to arrive and sit down. Then they filed in and took their places.

The brightly painted houses formed the backdrop, and the different animals sat by their houses with their pots and pans, waiting for the play to begin.

Once the rest of the children had arrived in the hall and sat down, the headteacher came onto the stage. “Quiet, everyone,” she said. “Today we are very lucky as we are going to see the play, ‘Why Anansi the Spider has Eight Thin Legs’, performed by Miss Beech’s class.”

Everyone clapped, and it was time to begin. The narrators introduced the play together in very loud voices.

The performance went very well and all of the children really enjoyed acting in the play and performing it for the rest of the school. At the end, the class stood in a line and bowed, as everyone clapped and cheered.
"That was brilliant," said Hinda. "I cannot wait to do another one!"